# The Slush Pile Demolitionist

*Les Zig*

First published in 2024 by ECG Press
www.ecgpress.com



ISBN
Paperback: 978-0-6454853-6-3
Ebook: 978-0-6454853-7-0

A Cataloguing-in-Publication entry for this book is available from the National Library of Australia.

# Contents

# Foreword

Les Zig is the best kept secret in Australian literature.

Perhaps it's because of his insistence on using pen names (Les Zig, Lazaros Zigomanis, Les Zigomanis) or how each of his books is so different from the last that he stubbornly defies categorisation, or even perhaps because the first letter of his surname ensures his work is inevitably found on the lowest shelf in the bookshop, where customers have to kneel on the floor, tilt their heads, and squint to find it; for whatever reason, his novels and stories, while enjoying some success, have not as yet enjoyed as much success as they should. This sentiment may be something that all writers feel in their hearts about their own work (I know I do!) but in Les Zig's case, as the stories in this collection show, it just so happens to be true.

"The Slush Pile Demolitionist," "Promotion" and "Requiem Me" form a hugely entertaining triptych of stories about writing. Writing about writing is difficult; all too often it can result in pomposity and bathos. Les is too skilled a writer to fall into those traps. His writers and editors are flawed, egotistical, selfish, funny, and sometimes even murderous. (Les has obviously known a lot of writers.) Yet at the same time, there remains something admirable about these characters, as they struggle to find success in a world that doesn't value them or their work, and that not only often rewards mediocrity over talent, but doesn't appear to even see a difference. As a writer, I nod to myself as I read these stories; as a reader, I simply enjoy them.

After reading this book, you too will be in on the secret I mentioned, if you aren't already.

Les Zig is a great writer.

Ryan O'Neill
*The Drover's Wives* (Brio Books 2018)
*Their Brilliant Careers* (Black Inc. 2016)
*The Weight of the Human Heart* (Black Inc. 2012)

# The Slush Pile Demolitionist

Constance Towers wasn't what I expected from a senior editor at a boutique publisher. In her gaudy pea poncho, faded pink jeans and open-toed sandals, she might've been a thrift shopper. Her small face was lost in a mass of stringy coppery hair, her eyes magnified behind a pair of oversized violet square-rimmed glasses. She might've been as young as twenty-five and as old as forty-five, some timeless literary nymph who now held me in her scrutiny.

"So you're studying …?" she asked from behind her pitted oak desk.

Her office was books: books on bookshelves, piled in teetering towers on the floor, and crammed on the windowpane; and manuscripts – bound, unbound, and fanned – on her desk and filing cabinets and the small aquarium with its kaleidoscopic collection of fish.

"Professional Writing and Publishing," I told her.

"Do you see yourself in publishing?"

"I'd love to make it as a writer. *Obviously.*"

Just in case it wasn't obvious. I'd written novels, short stories, articles, and even a couple of screenplays – the lot of them now yellowing in my old rusty filing cabinet. In the vacuum a lack of success had created, and with growing dissatisfaction over my job (floor clerk at a tech warehouse) my partner had encouraged that, at the ripe age of thirty-five, I go back to school and study – learn to put my skills to another use.

"But I feel I have the talent and experience to become an editor," I said.

School had recommended me for this post: a two-week placement with Veracity Publishing, a small indie publisher known for their literary fare. Veracity had probably chosen me due to my marks (I don't want to boast – they're all high distinctions), but, still, I felt woefully out of my depth.

"Veracity Publishing is dedicated to producing bold and innovative work," Constance said. "Perhaps you're familiar with some of the authors we've discovered?"

"Oh yeah," I said. "Abdul Khatri, Penelope Christakis, Skip Lago, Eno Mizden, Karin McCain …"

We'd talked about these authors at school. Except for Eno Mizden, the others had enjoyed such success they'd eventually jumped to bigger publishers for the money and the fame – what many consider to be *the dream*. While such rewards were attractive bonuses, they weren't why I wrote. I was still trying to work *that* out.

"We're actually working on Eno Mizden's new manuscript," Constance said. "Perhaps you'd be interested in reading it after you've settled in?"

"Sure."

"Well," Constance said, "Mr. Stiegler isn't here this week."

Stiegler was *the* boss. The prospect of facing him was daunting – meeting the boss for the first time always was. Constance was intimidating enough.

"But he left a note here suggesting we find a bit of reading for you to do." She rose from her chair. "Do you know what I mean about *reading*?"

"The slush pile?"

"Exactly – our unsolicited submissions. We're one of the few remaining publishers who still have a slush pile."

She led me from her small, cluttered office to the equally cluttered main floor. The six desks whined for mercy under a deluge of paperwork, boxy old computers, and personal knickknacks. The walls were just bookshelves overflowing with a combination of musty classics and Veracity's fare. Colorful pot plants were scattered throughout in some hopeless grasp of feng shui, although all they succeeded in doing was kill what little space remained.

We picked our way through to the desk in the furthest corner. The pièce de résistance to the clutter was a mountain of big yellow envelopes that constituted the slush pile. I wanted to plant a flag in it and declare it Mount Slushmore. Of course, a flag would mean I'd conquered it, and I doubted that was going to happen.

"It's not that hard." Constance grabbed one of the envelopes. "We still request hardcopy submissions – people get lazy with email. If they're going to submit to us, we want them to put effort in. Shows us they're serious."

Tearing open the envelope, she took out the submission. She mustn't have found what she looking for, as she put the manuscript down on the desk, and checked another envelope. Same outcome. Then another envelope. Now she flicked through the pages of the manuscript.

"What do you notice?" she asked.

The lines of text were tightly packed, which wasn't what you were meant to do when submitting to a publisher. You're meant to have space, for easy reading and so the reader can make notes if needed. Also, the author had used a Sans Serif font, like Arial – another no-no. Sans Serif fonts don't have little tails on the letters the way Serif fonts do. The belief is those little tales form an unseen line across the page that makes it easier to read. When submitting to a publisher, you're meant to use a Serif font.

I relayed my observations.

"Right. Our website lists the necessary submission requirements. From immediate appearances, this manuscript has failed to meet two of the criteria on our checklist." Constance found the accompanying stamped self-addressed envelope and shoved the submission into it. "Ditch it."

"Is that fair?"

"Fair?" Constance snorted. "If they can't do us the courtesy of meeting our guidelines, why should we do them the courtesy of reading their submission?"

"What if it's a masterpiece?"

"The writing life's tough."

"What do I say? 'Bad luck'?"

"We have a form rejection," Constance told me. "Have you seen one before?"

Now *I* almost snorted. I'd seen *hundreds*. What's worse was that they used your own stamped self-addressed envelope (another submission requirement – you've got to stick a stamped self-addressed envelope in with your submission) to be the harbinger of your failure. It's like putting a loaded gun in the hand of the guy thinking of murdering you.

"I've seen a few," I said.

"If the submission deserves more than a form rejection," Constance went on, "feel free to improvise. Just be tactful. Otherwise, read enough to get a feel for a piece, write a paragraph on what they're about, why they do or don't work, and whether they're worth pursuing or not. If you like anything, come talk to me. Any questions?"

"Am I qualified for this?"

"Qualified? It's *reading*."

Constance laughed once, shortly but loudly, then turned and headed back to her office.

## Week One: Tuesday

I wanted to find THE NEXT BIG THING so that I could live vicariously through some unknown's success, and show myself that it *could* happen. It might be a one in a million chance, a one in a billion chance, but it *was* a chance.

And it could be an inspiration.

Only I spent Monday wading through drivel.

After I'd read each sub, I'd knock out a paragraph-long report on my computer. When the reading got too much, I scribbled in my work-placement journal – a school requirement – to break up the humdrum.

Tuesday morning was little different.

Worse, the subs were unending. Constance came around and dumped a whole stack of new submissions on my desk. How many people were writing? And submitting? So it was read, *read*, **read**.

After lunch, I wearily picked up the next sub, a thriller entitled *In From the Cold*. The first chapter was okay (yay!), introducing a spy who'd been excommunicated, but had been asked back to deal with—

That's when it happened.

Turning the page too quickly, I tore it.

I blinked.

I shouldn't have been concerned. The page could be reprinted, but what did it say about the publisher if they were so careless with a submission? I was surprised to find I was oblivious to the fact that I was, indeed, oblivious.

The extreme response would be to retype the page, trying to match the font (possibly **Georgia** or something equally accessible) and the margins (also standard). I could photocopy the page; that would work, although photocopied pages always look like photocopies – particularly compared to originals. Or I could just leave the page as it was.

They were all workable options.

I contemplated them as I finished reading the submission. What started promisingly deteriorated rapidly into twaddle. The writing grew loose, the grammar problematic, and the plot became a rip-off of James Bond, including a double-x designation for spies licensed to kill, a superior known simply as "Ma'am", and a technology quartermaster known as "QM". It was so pleasingly bad it informed what I did next.

I scrunched up the torn page, tossed it in the bin, recompiled the rest of the manuscript, and stuck it in the accompanying stamped self-addressed envelope. I imagined what the author would think when he went through his manuscript and found a page missing.

He mightn't make this discovery for weeks, if not months, or even years. Maybe he'd even keep sending out the same hardcopy, completely unaware of the missing page. One day, though, he would find it. And what would he think? That the missing page was the cause of the manuscript being rejected? That he'd unwittingly self-sabotaged?

I finished the form rejection (which only required me inserting the author's name, and the title of the submission), printed out a copy, sat back, and looked at the slush pile with a new appreciation.

# Week One: Wednesday

Dear Tom,

His name was Tim but what better way to shatter him immediately? Particularly given I could pass it off as a typo.

> Thank you for your recent letter enclosing your manuscript.

Even better. The letter was personalized, but the rejection was form.

> We have viewed and considered your manuscript.

I read a chapter and a half.

> Unfortunately, we have decided not to make an offer of publication.

Not unfortunate for us, but for Tom – I mean Tim.

> Thank you once again for writing to us and we wish you every success in placing your manuscript elsewhere.

*I cannot believe how bad your manuscript is*, I would've liked to have written.

So much of Mount Slushmore's bounty read as indulgent – authors so misguided by the belief of their own genius that they put little work into their craft, and less into revision. They read like first drafts a sixth-grader had peddled out the night before homework was due to be turned in.

I knew this with certainty because I'd once had the same outlook – that the brilliance of my concepts would mesmerize the reader so they'd overlook the shoddy prose, appalling execution, and stream of tpyos. It must've been a rite of maturation as a writer. Now I revised endlessly (only to be equally unsuccessful, but at least I could take some pride in the writing, Impostor Syndrome aside).

Reading all this drivel incited an indignation in me that I didn't so much embrace, but immersed myself in. How could these be the writers I was competing against? Surely I wasn't on this level. Surely, there were better writers. As much as I wanted to crush the bad writers, I wanted to find something that I could exalt.

Something that could *wow* me.

Something that could – and *would* – be my hope.

## Week One: Thursday

Constance liked mismatching: today, green corduroys, a black vest, and a silk lavender shirt with puffy shoulders. Her shoes were the identical type, but one was a fluorescent green, and the other a bloody red. It was easy to underestimate her because she didn't fit the stereotype of some exec. But now I ascertained an artfulness behind it, a cleverly constructed ruse designed to encourage people to underestimate her.

"Come with me," she told me.

"Where?" I asked.

But she was already off, forcing me to jump up and canter to catch up.

"We spoke about Eno Mizden the day you arrived," she said.

Eno Mizden was a poster boy for students and faculty at school – a writer and poet (funny how those two things aren't synonymous) carving out a niche in the literary community. He'd come to talk at an industry function once:

a jittery coat rack with a disproportionately big larynx who was typically, if not predictably Goth – dark, depressing, doomed. Facsimiles swarmed the hallways of school – peons to a stereotype. They weren't poets. They were peots. I used to wear black to be cool – or to at least try to be. The peots were the reason I stopped.

Veracity Publishing had picked Eno's sub from the slush pile five years ago. That debut novel and the follow up had been critical successes that had placed well in awards and heralded Eno as a talent for the future.

"Have you read either of his books?" Constance asked.

Eno wrote *literary* fiction – angst-ridden characters coming to grips with being so angsty while trying to find their place in the world, although couched in densely pretentious prose that was common to bad literary fiction. I mean, the good writers can do it – their prose is sophisticated and beautifully constructed. You can spend hours examining the meaning behind sentences. The wannabes construct flowery pastiches that laughably unravel under inspection. I preferred *genre* fiction – heroes saving the world and stuff like that.

"Um, no," I said.

We exited the Veracity loft and weaved our way through the parking lot to Constance's battered red Volkswagen. She didn't pick up the conversation again until she'd reversed out of her spot as if it had catapulted her; she then honked her way into the busy morning traffic.

"We're working on Eno's third book," she said. "We're hoping this will be the one."

"The one?" I asked.

"That sells. Regardless of our commitment to the literary community, we still need to make money. We keep hoping Eno's commercial recognition will catch-up with his critical cache."

"Everybody at school loves him," I said. "They think he's gritty."

"He's a whorethur."

"A what?"

"A writer who professes artistic merit, but he lives for that effect. He hasn't sold out for money; he's sold out to be a starving artist."

"So what's the purpose of this meeting?"

"Eno's been pestering us for feedback. He's not very secure – most writers aren't."

*You got that right!* I almost exclaimed.

"Their books are their children they send defenseless into the world," Constance went on. "This meeting is to stroke Eno's ego. God knows he needs it. If Eno detects a hint of negativity, he'll jump out a window."

"You serious?"

Constance rolled her eyes.

"Should I be coming to this thing?"

"It'll be educational."

"In how to handle authors?"

"That, and in what you *shouldn't* become."

Fifteen minutes later, we were sitting in a train carriage of a bookshop-café. Tatty tan shades covered the windows so everything had a sepia tint. On a stage at the front, a slam poet pounded out a nonsensical poem about oppression, although I bet her background was middle-class suburbia. The patrons were as worn and patchwork as the second-hand books scattered on the tables and shelves. Watching the poet, their eyes gleamed with the mindless zeal of cultists.

We were punctual but Eno Mizden wasn't, so Constance asked me about my writing. I told her about the stuff I'd written, stashed away in my filing cabinet, and she told me to take my best work, and submit it to Veracity. I said I would but didn't tell her that I'd submitted my best work – *Crimson Dreams Waking* – to a commercial publisher a few months ago. I'd sent them three chapters, then they'd requested to see the whole thing. Off went my bulky yellow envelope – hopefully to discover a new world.

When Eno arrived, I noted he was even thinner than the last time I'd seen him at the school industry talk. His shoulders and elbows were bulbous knobs in his black shirt, and the prong of his belt poked through a homemade puncture – the third such puncture after all the regular holes. The only thing that had any health was his lustrous spiky black hair (that I'm guessing had been dyed from some pedestrian shade of brown), and eye-liner that was meant to show what an INDIVIDUAL he was. When Constance introduced me as an editorial assistant, he gave me the sort of look people reserve for finding an unflushed turd in a public toilet.

"Eno, you're looking great," Constance said.

"Thanks," he said in a tone that suggested he knew he was being handled, but he smiled nonetheless – the phony bastard.

That's when I saw them. They peeked out from under the cuffs of his black sleeves – thin white scars on his thin white wrists. Not just one on each either; they crisscrossed, suggesting he'd taken to his wrists repeatedly, although not with any gusto.

"*Life in a Bloodshot World*," Constance said, "is great."

"Really?" Eno's voice trembled.

Here was his quandary: he *wanted* and *needed* the praise, but would always doubt it. I knew that feeling.

"It's marvelous," Constance said.

*Marvelous*! It's such a fake word. Nothing's marvelous. Not even the word marvelous.

"And the title …" Constance said. "Have I told you this before?"

"No, no, no," Eno said.

"It's the embodiment of the struggles you write about. I don't know how you came up with it."

"Well," Eno paused theatrically, drawing out the anticipation of an obvious punch line, "I did have to do a lot of research."

Then he guffawed this great seesawing laughter like his mouth was trying to eat his own head.

For the next fifteen minutes, Constance mindlessly praised *Bloodshot World*. Eno would've had to be an idiot to not know he was being flattered (although I didn't discount the possibility), but he lapped it up like the unrelenting phony he was.

The meeting ended with handshakes, a smile from Eno in my direction – the unsightly turd had been flushed (or perhaps he'd just closed the lid on it) – and the promise that Stiegler would meet with him the following week.

## Week One: Friday

I read *Life in a Bloodshot World* last night – a pretentious exploration of the suffering of everyday people as imagined by an equally pretentious Gothic charlatan.

I couldn't imagine the book selling in any meaningful numbers, although it was so indecipherably and hideously ostentatious that most reviewers would be afraid to criticize it just in case it was THE NEXT BIG THING. They'd continue to trumpet Eno as an important literary voice.

Going into Veracity, I was looking forward to the unassuming bunk of the slush pile purifying me of Eno's putrescence but Constance, waiting at my desk, had other ideas.

"Did you read *Life in a Bloodshot World*?" she asked.

"Yeah."

"Do you know what a media release is?"

"An overview of the book for the media and reviewers."

"Have you ever written one?"

"Nope."

"Let's give the slush pile a rest for the morning," Constance said.

*Give the slush pile a rest? What about me? The slush pile never tires!*

Constance accessed Veracity's network drive from my computer and opened several files. "These are examples of media releases," she said. "They're not complicated. Copy the format and apply it to *Bloodshot World*."

"I didn't really like the book," I told her.

"In publishing, you're not always going to work on books you *like*. Do your best."

She smiled and left me at it.

After several false starts, I knocked out half of a first draft.

### Summary

A spurious, if not disingenuous insight into the everyday fears and insecurities of everyday people, *Life in a Bloodshot World* will appeal to conceited morons who'll read it simply for the bragging rights that they've done so. It'll complete their meaningless little lives in meaningless little ways, allowing them to regale meaningless little friends at meaningless little social gatherings with *Bloodshot World's* quasi-enlightened drivel.

This effort provided the foundation for my second draft:

### Summary

*Life in a Bloodshot World* offers a telling insight into the everyday fears and insecurities of ordinary people. Honest, confronting, and enlightening, *Bloodshot World* is a gripping and brutal parable that unrelentingly assaults us with the everyday problems we must all face, and the extremes to which they may push us.

*Bloodshot World* is about a married couple with a seven-year-old son and a five-year-old daughter. The father's an alcoholic, a gambler, and questioning his sexuality, while his lush wife faces (what she sees as) the stagnation of her life. Trapped by kids, housework, and domesticity, she trolls the slums engaging in seedy trysts. Her husband frequents gay bars, chats up gay men, but then always anxiously retreats before anything can happen. Then, in the final chapter, he has sex with his male boss on the boss's desk – there's no set up for it. It just happens.

But that's the whole book. Nothing's set up or justified. Things occur because they need to so the story can keep moving to where it needs to go with predictable monotony.

I could see now why Constance referred to Eno Mizden as a whorethur.

Finishing the media release, I printed it out and took it to Constance. She skimmed it, then nodded.

"Excellent!" she said. "If you don't make it as a writer, or in publishing, you can always try copywriting."

I wasn't sure how to take that.

## Saturday and Sunday

If you haven't been able to tell, a restlessness has crept into my life. It has nothing to do with my family. My partner has always been supportive, and our three pre-teen kids are great kids. Our husky, although she's getting on, is a character herself.

But now, when I sat in front of the computer to write, I couldn't find the words. The slush pile reflected my own hopes. Maybe I just wasn't good enough – maybe I was just like all those poor saps I rejected. Or, worse, maybe I'd just *never* be good enough.

Of course, a publisher requested my full manuscript.

But what did that mean? I could remain *thereabouts* forever. If that was the case, what came next? As much as I love my wife and family, what else existed for me? The chase of publication used to excite me. Now it elicited growing hopelessness.

My partner was much more optimistic about the prospect of my manuscript being requested than I was.

I was guarded.

I didn't want to go *all-in*, like this was the only hand I had remaining.

But it *was* beginning to feel the way.

## Week Two: Monday

If you took Santa Claus out of his red costume and plonked him in a tweed suit and a leather beret, that would be Stiegler. His thinning snowy hair had been tied back into a ponytail. His black shoes were obscenely pointed, like they'd been designed for kicking holes in walls or something.

He swept in this morning, exchanging jovial greetings with everybody. The dread I felt had less to do with him and more to do with the expectation that soon, I'd have to meet him – the *boss*.

I buried my head in Mount Slushmore.

The submissions kept coming in. No wonder so many publishers stopped accepting unsolicited stuff.

I was meant to read *enough* to get a feel for a submission. Sometimes, this meant I had to read all of it (a cover letter, a synopsis, and three chapters). Other times, I didn't have to venture so deeply.

As was the case, for example, with *A Hero's Journey, and Back Again*, a fantasy epic (well, an *intended* epic).

It began:

*A Hero's Journey, and Back Again*

## Chapter One

After years in the West, the hero Trebor finally returned to the homes of his fathers. A hero of quests beyond count, Trebor had fought heroically in wars and crusades. A lesser man, a lesser hero, may have succumbed – if not to the physical ardors of battle, then to the psychological deterioration encouraged by death and despair. But one thought had always sustained Trebor: Eitalan. She was his love, his life, a reason to live. Without her, Trebor knew he never would've found the trength *[sic]* to be a hero.

That was as much as I needed to cobble together my report:

**A Hero's Journey, and Back Again**
Underwhelming fantasy fare featuring Trebor, who is apparently a hero, his journeys into the lands of the West, and the battles he must fight and quests he must achieve before he can be with his one true love, Eitalan. Poorly written.

What I didn't glean from the paragraph I read, I got from the synopsis provided with the manuscript.

If you think such a snap judgement was horrible, consider this:

MOVING FORWARD

1. LISA

Lisa was a zany

Zany? *Really*? That immediately prejudiced me against the story. (The rest of the submission, fortunately, made a good case for prejudices.)

A trinkling of submissions, however, verged on good, leaving me thinking that with lots of sympathetic editing they could be something. That's all some of these writers needed: *guidance*.

And a chance.

I took one sub I somewhat enjoyed to Constance – a story of magical realism where a beleaguered homemaker begins believing she's a sorceress, and eventually discovers she's a Witch Queen from another dimension who was hidden as a child on Earth to protect her from enemies who'd wiped out her family.

Constance read it while I waited, nodding every now and again and offering an encouraging, "Hmmm", saw the potential, then told me it would need too *much* nurturing.

"You can tell the writer's not quite there yet with their craft," she said. "It'd take years of going back and forth to get it to a publishable standard. We just don't have the resources unfortunately. But maybe, one day, the writer will get there themselves. *Maybe.*"

So I went back to my desk and rejected.

Rejected. Rejected. Rejected.

Between the arbitrary rejections and the sabotage, I became a petty despot intoxicated with power, qualifying it with the rationale that *when* I did find something good I *would* kick it up.

## Week Two: Tuesday

A big shadow fell over me and Mount Slushmore. I thought it was Constance with another deposit of submissions. Nope. Stiegler. We'd missed one another yesterday. Presumably, he was busy catching up on everything – well, hopefully not *everything*.

His scrutiny was, in itself, inscrutable – this inexplicable thing that running his own publishing house had abstracted. How well had he learned to read people? Did he know what I'd been doing? Was he wondering how this mature-age student was surpassing the reading quota met by his previous readers?

"You want to come into my office?" he asked.

His office was bigger than Constance's, and bare other than for an oak desk, the phone, a Mac laptop, and two chairs. It was an exercise in minimalism, so clean and streamlined that it felt that I had not only entered a different building, but a different plane of existence. This might've been literary purgatory.

Stiegler gestured for me to sit down, and then took his own seat – one of those ergonomic recliners that had probably been made especially for him.

"So," Stiegler said, "tell me about yourself."

*For the last week, I've been culling your slush pile!*

"I'm a writer," I said, plummeting into the spiel I delivered whenever I met new people, "although an unsuccessful one."

"An unsuccessful writer!" Stiegler chuckled, like this was an archetype with which he was not only familiar, but very good friends with. Of course, given he ran Veracity, I'm sure he had the archetype over on such a regular basis it was now a cliché. "What do you write?" he asked.

"There's nothing I haven't written over the years – novels, screenplays, stories, articles," I said. "I've had a few little things published and nibbles at some of the bigger stuff."

I waited for a prompt, but when none came, I had to elaborate.

"I mean, I haven't had much luck." *Any luck, actually!* "But I still send stuff out."

"I was a writer once myself," Stiegler said. "Not very good, mind you. I didn't have the passion to keep writing – that insatiable need to tell my stories. Do you know what I mean?"

I nodded. Yes, I knew very well what he meant.

"But I understand the nature of submission, and the requirement of perseverance. You should submit something to us."

"Constance said the same thing."

"You'll find this is often the way publishing works – it's sometimes a case of *who* you know. We're getting two weeks of free labor out of you. I'm sure we can offer something in return. In any case, don't be discouraged. You're still young."

"I'm five years older than Eno Mizden."

"Your circumstances differ. I understand you're married, have children, and a job – Eno's been single his whole life, and only needed to work sporadically. Then there's. well ..." Stiegler *harrumphed*, although I couldn't tell whether the sound was derision or amusement. "Some people literally blunder into luck, like they'd stepped in a pile of dog shit on a morning walk, while others make their own. Eno was lucky – right time, right place, right ... *tone* of work. Still, he's never captured the market the way we would've liked."

*Understandable given he writes pretentious crap!*

Stiegler's phone rang. He glanced at it and arched his brows. "Speak of the devil," he said. "Excuse me." He picked up the phone. "Eno! How're you?"

Eno's voice on the other end sounded like the indecipherable babble they used to give adults in the old Charlie Brown cartoons.

"You have to excuse me, Eno," Stiegler said, "but I was on a buying trip."

More spatter from Eno.

"Yes, yes, I'm reading it."

Obviously inquiring about his book – probably so he could have his ego stroked further. The bastard. Getting it from Constance hadn't been enough.

"No, no, let me finish it before I comment."

*But please, Mr. Stiegler*, I imagined Eno whining, *I'm such a worthless little ingrate. Please give me some praise. Pleaaaase!*

"Really, Eno, let's talk about it later this week."

*Awww! How will I survive? My life shall be a misery!*

"Very well. How about tomorrow? At that café in the city where we signed you?"

*Do they still let in bleak, moronic pretenders?*

"Yes, yes, Eno."

*Oh the joy! The thundercloud has lifted from my life! Please, Mr. Stiegler, put me down so that I may be miserable again!*

"Really, Eno, you'll just have to wait."

*Be harsher with me, pleeeaaaaaase, Mr. Stiegler!*

"If you'll excuse me, Eno, I am in a meeting. Midday, tomorrow."

*I'm going to sulk.*

"See you then."

*Sob. (I am happy again!)*

Stiegler hung up the phone. "I'm sorry about that."

"That's okay."

"To get back to the point I was going to make: things change." I was astounded how easily he could resume the thread of our conversation. "Or *you* change them," he added.

"Me?" My paranoia spiked. Was he referring to my work on Mount Slushmore?

"It may be cliché, but we make our own fate."

"Oh." I don't think Shakespeare could've written a more appropriate response.

"So, tell me, why Professional Writing and Publishing?"

"After trying to make it as a writer for so long, I thought I had talents that could be applicable to the industry."

Stiegler's eyes narrowed. He knew a line. "What sort of talents?"

"Editing." I wanted to leave it at that, but Stiegler's gaze compelled me to yield something more. "I think I know how to put a story together, how to make it work, how to revise it so that it realizes its fullest potential."

That was my favorite term at school: *realize its fullest potential.* It's what I told students who submitted to the school journal when I was editor – *I just want your piece to realize its fullest potential.* And I did. I truly did. It's how I would justify my reams of feedback.

Still, Stiegler didn't blink.

"So, yeah," I said, again feeling the need to fill the silence, "editing."

Stiegler arched one bushy eyebrow, the thing going up like it was a meter measuring just how much crap I could talk.

"And how've you found the course?"

"It's good," I said.

Again, the silence. It was like an empty pool on a hot day: it just had to be filled.

"I mean, I think I had a pretty good grasp of things going into the course, but I've learned stuff." I left it hanging, hoping Stiegler would move on. He didn't. The bastard. "Important stuff," I offered, but no good. Stiegler still kept quiet. *The bastard.* "And it's good talking to like-minded people. It's like, when I was at high school, I was always the loner, the weird kid, I think because I wanted to be a writer. While everybody else was doing teenage stuff, I was reading, or lost in my imagination, wanting to write stories." *Stop me please!* "But now it's like a whole school full of people like me." *Well, not just like me, but close enough.* "I guess maybe I'm surprised by the talent of some of them. And, to think, there'll be more next year, and the year after that, and so on."

"Constance tells me you've done wonders with the slush pile."

*I've done something all right!*

"Um, thanks," I said.

"She's impressed by your reports," Stiegler went on. "She thinks they show real insight. However, you haven't kicked anything up for consideration."

"I … just … haven't … really read anything," I said, now conscious not to speak too slowly, too quickly, or too incriminatingly, "which deserved it. I showed Constance one. She said the standard needed to be higher."

"Indubitably. Eno's first book is, in fact, the last slush pile submission we accepted, and that was five years ago."

The percentages of that acceptance almost made me shudder.

"Could you see yourself working in an office like this?"

I hated myself for thinking it, but is this where people went when they didn't make it? Like that old saying, *Those who can, do. Those who can't, teach.* Would landing in a job like this be a capitulation? It was a lofty thought I wanted to crush as arrogant, but it scared me all the same.

"I guess," I said. "I'm not really used to office life."

"I think you'd excel," Stiegler said. "Think about it."

"Thanks."

Stiegler got up and thrust his hand across the table. "It's been a pleasure to meet you."

I rose and shook his hand. "You, too, sir."

And meant it.

## Week Two: Wednesday

Numerous little cafes and restaurants shared the same alley promenade. You couldn't tell which sets of tables belonged to what establishment. And it was so packed I got a sense of everything and everybody around us closing in. Poor Eno bobbed at our table like a pathetic windsock. But Stiegler beamed, as if the lunchtime hubbub powered him.

Eno's manuscript – the pages curling, the corners dog-eared, Stiegler's keys sitting on top as a paperweight – was nestled among our empty plates and glasses, arguably the most unpalatable thing on the table.

"I've been worrying," Eno said, once we'd finished eating and the pleasantries were out of the way.

"Worrying?" Stiegler asked.

"About the book."

"You always worry." Stiegler turned to me and chortled. "He always worries. Such a perfectionist."

"So you like it then?" Eno asked.

"Eno! Eno! Eno!"

Eno leaned forward, the way a puppy might try to coax a caress from its owner.

"Eno, this," Stiegler said, "this is … "

"Yes, Mr. Stiegler, yes …?"

" … just not good enough."

"Not good enough?"

"While it brims with potential, in its current state it's too self-important and dense."

Eno slumped, a scarecrow who'd just had its stuffing ripped out. The weirdest thing was the fist-pumping elation I felt.

"Constance said it was going wonderfully!"

"Miss Towers is a soft touch. Let's talk realities: your last two books? Everybody loved them, nobody bought them. We need a book everybody loves, and everybody buys. Actually, I'd even settle for a book that nobody loves, but everybody buys. This," Stiegler drummed the manuscript, "is, frankly, *lacking*."

Eno jumped to his feet (and would've upended his chair, had he any real weight) and skittered away. I kept waiting for the wind to blow him back, but I guess even the wind had taste. Eno scooted around the corner.

I expected Stiegler to be stern and condemning, but he smiled until the color rose in his cheeks.

"Yes?" he said.

"It's not *that* bad," I said. "It's not something I'd read, and it's pretentious, but you're making out like it's the worst thing ever."

"Damnit," Stiegler said, "it's adequate!" Now he stroked the manuscript, like it was a cat purring contentedly in his lap.

"*Adequate?*"

"Eno's work has grown increasingly self-important. It's a façade that has to be demolished. Behind it, well … it's workable."

"But you treated him so …?"

"Atrociously? Viciously? Condescendingly?" Stiegler bellowed uproariously with laughter. "He's an author. They all need to be treated differently." His grin broadened until it threatened to split his face in two, but the expression was forced – a mimicry. Here was a man who might've failed at writing fiction, yet perpetrated the greatest fiction of them all – that he was empathetic. "We've coddled Eno, and for what? Eno feigns sufferance, but he plays that for marquee. He's not a starving artist; he inherited his house and a comfortable nest egg from his parents. He could give it all up, but then he'd genuinely face a struggling existence. He doesn't want that. So perhaps he needs a dose of reality to find the verisimilitude his writing requires. Anyway, he's contracted."

"Sorry?"

"Just in case you're worried that he'll flee to another publisher."

I wasn't.

"He's contracted for three books," Stiegler said, "and damn him, we'll have that third book!"

## Week Two: Thursday

Bulky yellow envelope.

But it didn't belong to Mount Slushmore.

It poked out of my mailbox slot, like an impudent tongue mocking me.

Bulky yellow envelopes meant only one thing: *rejection*. If the publisher had accepted my manuscript, they'd call me. Or email me. They wouldn't be returning my manuscript in that death warrant of a yellow envelope.

I snatched it out of the mailbox and tore it open. There was no dread, no anticipation, no anything. Years ago, my heart would race, my hands would tremble, and I'd pause before opening the envelope, savoring the possibility of success. Time, rejection, and repetition had destroyed that excitement.

My eyes went straight to the body of the text:

> Thank you for giving us the opportunity to consider your manuscript.
>
> We read it with interest but I regret that we will not be making an offer of publication. We do not feel we are the right firm to successfully publish this book.
>
> Thank you for thinking of us, and we wish you every success in finding a publisher for your work.

Two *thank yous* to neuter my hopes. He must've enjoyed doing it, the bastard. I inferred bliss in every word.

And sure, here was the moment I could've had an epiphany empathizing with the author of my rejection letter, this moment of enlightenment acknowledging what I'd been doing and repent or whatever, but it didn't happen.

I went into Veracity. Mount Slushmore was bigger today, but now it didn't seem as unconquerable.

Today, I was planting my flag.

## Week Two: Friday

"Well?"

Stiegler. I sat opposite him in his office. He was nothing but unflinching sternness now. He might've been a judge weighing up the merits of delivering the death penalty to a hapless defendant.

"Would you care to explain your work on the slush pile?" he said.

Yesterday, I'd gauged submissions solely on instinct, an artiste who'd used all forms of munitions – instinctively evaluating the competency of the prose, the word choices, the name *choices*, the shape of the text on the page, the font used – to blow the crap out of the slush pile.

I'd wanted to find that *one* quality submission that would reaffirm my dreams. Stiegler had said the last slush pile submission they'd accepted was Eno's first book, and he was a fake. That was *not* what I wanted. There had to be something *real*.

Stiegler's phone rang. I jolted. Stiegler remained unmoved. His phone continued to ring. He picked it up and listened.

"Wait," he said. "I'll be right there."

Relief. *He'd be right there*, which meant—

"Come with me," Stiegler said.

"What?"

Stiegler led me to his tan Merc in the parking lot. The model had to be twenty years old, but was as close to pristine as maintenance would allow. An air-freshener, shaped like a pine tree, hung from the rearview mirror, the scent cloying.

"Where are we going?" I asked.

Stiegler started the car, the engine purring to life – sorry, cliché, but I couldn't help it in my frazzled state.

"Eno's having problems," he said.

"What sort of problems?"

"*Problems*," Stiegler said, navigating the car into busy, early morning traffic.

I wanted to push it – not because I was interested in Eno, but because it would mean we were talking about anything *but* what I'd done. But I didn't have the courage to try Stiegler's mood. So we said nothing for the first fifteen minutes as Stiegler drove into the leafy inner suburbs, our only accompaniment some opera that played from the stereo (the LCD display identified it as Wagner's "Gotterdammerung"). I'd just started to feel the littlest bit comfortable when Stiegler took a deep breath, like he was cocking his mouth to fire a barrage.

"Veracity Publishing stands for something," he said. "We want to enhance our literary culture. We want to look outside mainstream avenues and promote innovation and originality. The slush pile is one of our best resources to discover brave new authors."

*Brave new authors? What do they do? Fight lions?* But the thought had no wit. The air freshener's scent grew nauseating.

"Obviously, working one's way through the slush pile is daunting," Stiegler said. "It's the age of computers. The internet. Blogs. Social media.

Idiots telling us what they do daily, what they think hourly, whatever comes into their head, whoring themselves for fleeting gratification. Everybody thinks they're a creative. Worse, every home has a computer, so it's much easier to write and submit to a publisher. That means that every slush pile reader has to find their own way of dealing with the volume of material."

Here it was. There was no escaping this.

"You got through quite a bit of the slush pile yesterday," Stiegler said.

I tried to think of a way to justify my expediency, but nothing sounded believable.

"Constance has been auditing your work."

Stiegler slammed the brakes; I was thrown forward in my seat and lassoed back in by the seatbelt.

"Get out," he said.

Before I could ask why, he was out of the car with surprising nimbleness. I unbuckled the seatbelt, opened the door, and – dizzy, nauseous, and uncoordinated – fell out of the car and onto my knees, expecting a mob-like hit. Dictionary to the back of the head. *Bang!* So this was the crime for defiling the slush pile.

Damn, these independent publishers were unforgiving.

But Stiegler moved away from me. We'd pulled up outside a house – one of those squat brick affairs that were boxed-in alongside every other house on a street teeming with weeping willows and scattered leaves.

Stiegler was at the front door, ringing the bell and calling out, "Eno?"

Nothing.

Stiegler gestured for me to join him.

I trudged through the yard, hauling the burden of my guilt behind me. Bizarrely, the guilt wasn't for what I'd done, but that I'd been caught – the lament of so many criminals.

"Eno?" Stiegler said again, as he now not only rung the bell, but also thumped on the door. But still no answer. He tried the doorknob. It turned. He swung the door open, then stopped.

As I arrived on the porch, I saw why.

Two streams of blood stole down the length of the hallway's floorboards.

"We should call the police—" I said, but Stiegler was already on the way in.

I didn't want to follow, and even made a conscious decision not to, but there I was, tiptoeing behind Stiegler. He moved with surety; morbid fascination drove me. The blood ran from an archway leading into what turned out to be the lounge room.

The décor was old – gaudy green velvet couches, a mahogany coffee table on a pastiche woolly rug, and a line of family photos on the mantel above the fireplace. Various vases, lamps, and ceramic knickknacks sat on end tables. It wasn't the room of a Gothic writer who'd struggled and suffered for his art, but a snapshot into the past – Eno's past of middle-class suburbia, replete with warmth, familiarity, and love.

A recliner faced the TV – the only two contemporary items in the room. On the recliner's armrest sat a thin, pale arm – Eno Mizden's arm. The wrist was slashed so deep that it exposed bone. Blood trickled from the wound and pooled upon the floor. I couldn't see the other wrist because of the recliner's backrest, but I guessed it must be the same given the second stream of blood.

Stiegler grabbed the recliner's headrest and spun the chair to reveal Eno Mizden. He was whiter than ever, his eyes frozen in curious astonishment. In his lap rested a disheveled printout of his manuscript. A bloody straight-razor sat on the cover page in a splotch of blood.

I imagined how it'd played out: Stiegler had shattered him the previous day – not just shattered his confidence, but *him*, Eno Mizden. So Eno came home and tried to reconcile his life and his work. Genuinely suffering, he manically worked on his manuscript until late last night. He printed it out and reread it, doubting the quality of every word. Come the morning, the insecurity was too much.

So Eno fetched his straight-razor. The scars emblazoned across his wrists rebuked him as a phony. This is his moment of clarity, when he realized everything he is, everything about him, is a lie. He picked up his phone – sitting on a small end-table adjacent to the recliner – rang Stiegler, and … what? I didn't know. But he indicated to Stiegler there was a problem. He wanted to show Stiegler that he was for real this time. Finally.

Then Eno hung up, cut himself to the bone, and bled to death.

"Call the police," Stiegler said.

"I don't know where we are."

Stiegler pulled out his phone and called the police as I sat on the couch. This was meant to be a work placement, and yet here I was unravelling – and had been unravelling, if I were honest, from the moment I'd walked into Veracity. Was this the end you faced when you made the wrong beginning? When you realized that everything you thought was real *wasn't* real at all?

The cops came, as did the paramedics, and even a few reporters, but Stiegler handled the lot so clinically they may have bored him. Maybe they did; maybe this was all in the fine print of his job description.

It was late afternoon before we were dismissed. Stiegler filched Eno's bloody manuscript, then drove us to Veracity to the same Wagner opera (it must've been on loop). The offices were empty – a relief. I didn't know if I could face anybody else right now.

In my absence, Mount Slushmore had grown. Good on it. There was one unassailable truth: people kept writing. They took their lives, their dreams, and their fantasies, and tried to wrestle them into a coherent narrative … for what? To tell their story? To share their story? For fame? Riches? Self-gratification? All of the above?

I kept doing it despite my lack of success and only now, in the wake of Eno's death, found it wasn't because I desired any of that, but I wanted to share and connect with people in a way I usually didn't.

Unlike Eno, I wanted to find that truth in myself.

"Sit down," Stiegler said.

I sat at my desk.

Stiegler planted Eno's manuscript on another desk, then wheeled out the chair – dodging around a pot plant full of purple and yellow pansies – so he could sit opposite me. He gestured at Mount Slushmore. So here it was – despite everything that happened today, I still had to face my crimes.

"You know," Stiegler said, although now he was quite conversational, "I was saying before, everybody's a writer. No matter what they do in life, no matter how capable they are, no matter how imaginative, they all try. Do you know what that means?"

"Lots more tripe?"

"Yes." Stiegler's voice was a gleeful whisper. "*Lots!* Somebody needs to be the silent guardian, the watcher at the door, the last vestige of quality control. Somebody needs to uphold literary integrity while the digital world drowns us in muck and shit and irrelevancies and shit and even more shit."

"Why bother with a slush pile at all, then?"

"Because there *will* be that diamond in the rough." Stiegler grinned – a caricature of joy that escalated into a combination of malice and relish. "I like your work on the slush pile. I like it *a lot*. It's not enough to reject these pretenders. They need to be discouraged. They need to be *stopped*. And, *you*, are doing that!"

"What if—?"

"No!" Stiegler jumped up so abruptly that his chair rolled back into the desk behind it. "Don't question it! The ones who want to write will keep coming back. They won't be able to help themselves. That's *who* writers are. Well, *genuine* writers. *True* voices. *You* know that, don't *you*?"

He was seeing inside me. Despite my rejection, despite my despondency, I *would* no doubt go through a period of self-pity and questioning of my worth but, invariably, I'd dust myself off and keep writing, keep submitting because that's who I was. I'd done it before, and I'd do it again.

"Let the pretenders fall," Stiegler said. "*You* just have to recognize the uncut gems."

"And if I get it wrong?"

"Leave that to marketing. You can sell anything if you want it bad enough and are prepared to make sacrifices."

*Sacrifices*. Like Eno? Had he been a sacrifice? His suicide would popularize his book, and be a launchpad into best-seller strata. People would buy his earlier books to examine if there was any hint of his deterioration. Had Stiegler manipulated Eno to this very result? Could he be that cold and calculating?

"Did I drive Eno to suicide?" Stiegler said. "That's what you're thinking."

I nodded slowly.

"What do you think?"

I couldn't believe anybody could be so heartless, but I'd caught those glimpses of

Stiegler's ruthlessness. Had I made more of them than they were? Or hadn't I feared them enough? Right now, I was too confused to make sense of it, but if I sorted through it I was sure I would find an answer.

The question was whether I wanted to face that answer.

I looked uncertainly at Eno's manuscript on the other desk.

Stiegler must've read my indecision. His eyes were unblinking as he nodded once.

"Your placement finishes today," he said, "but I want you to work for me when you finish your schooling. I can understand how this unfortunate experience might've soured you. But if not me, if not Veracity, I'm willing to recommend you to the publisher of your choice." He clapped me on the shoulder. "You've found your place. At least for now."

Smiling, he took Eno's manuscript, entered his office, and closed the door.

For a long time, I gaped after him.

Then I turned to the slush pile, opened an envelope, and began to read.

# Promotion

The promotion should've been mine!

The Associates implied they were going to choose me for the position of fiction publisher if I did a good job, if I put in the time, but instead they went with an outsider, with Ivan, Ivan (or *Eee-vun*, as he pronounced his name) Kerkow.

*Ivan Kerkow!*

I hadn't planned to kill him – really I hadn't. Oh, certainly, you can make a case that I cut the b-string from my piano; that I brought my tattered gardening gloves with the frayed hems in to work; that I wore my black jeans, a black jacket, and a gray shirt; and that I lay in wait, in the parking lot, enshrouded in darkness, surrounded by thickets, obscured by driving rain splattering on the glistening asphalt; but, really, I was only trying to feel self-important – anybody would do the same.

Then he emerged from the building's rear exit, this tiny thin man in an awful cream cardigan with patched elbows, whistling a merry tune and jingling his car keys as he made his way to his company car (a Beamer), a bounce in his step.

A *bounce!*

Next thing I knew, I had the piano string tightening around his neck – tightening so that it carved into his throat and sheared through flesh, muscle, and tendon. It felt – and sounded (for what muffled, grinding sound it made, and could be heard over his gurgling and gasping, our wrestling, as well as the pounding rain) – like leather ripping.

He couldn't scream, couldn't use that voice that had inexplicably impressed the Associates into choosing him over me. But he did struggle for what little it was worth, although I was too determined – as determined as I had been after they'd implied the promotion was mine.

Pain sliced into the bottom half of my right hand – the piano string had cut through my glove and was now doing to my poor hand what it was doing to the beastly Ivan's neck. Oh, the damn usurper. This horrible, thoughtless man. Would his inconsideration never end? First my promotion, then one of my favorite gardening gloves, and now my hand. How much more need I suffer?

Supported only by the piano string, his body slumped, a lifeless marionette now bereft of all ambition. I stood there a moment or two, reconciling what I'd done, until the sound of his keys falling from his limp grasp and hitting the ground startled me into action. Where to now? I had not considered this at all. But I was a senior editor and used to cleaning up messes, used to making something coherent and purposeful from something ungodly and directionless.

*The scene. I had to clear the scene!*

I went to my battered Ford and opened the boot, still filled with sacks of remaindered books. You see them on discount tables outside bookstores, beggars crying for a home before they are sent back to be pulped. I collected them periodically from the office with the intention of disposing of them but had not gotten around to it yet. Underneath them, I had a tarpaulin that I wrangled out and used to wrap up Ivan's body.

He was little, but heavy – *dense*, no doubt, with duplicity – as I dragged him to my car and deposited him into the boot only to find I didn't have the room. The backseat was an option, but risky. What if I was stopped? And why have him there anyway? Laying there reproachfully as I drove. Hadn't the damn usurper cost me enough?

The Beemer!

I recovered his keys, opened the boot, and slung him in there. He fit so perfectly it may have been where he always belonged. Then I drove to the bay, taking a scenic route – the Beemer was a beautiful car, and who knew whether I would ever have opportunity to drive another? It was just too good a motoring experience to abbreviate as I had abbreviated Ivan.

When I arrived at my destination, I removed Ivan from the boot, unwrapped the tarpaulin enough to weigh him down with rocks from the bank, wrapped him back up like a book in a dust jacket, and rolled him into the bay. There. Gone. Just like a manuscript deleted with a single keystroke.

Now for the Beemer.

For one irrational moment, I contemplated keeping it. Why not? It should've been mine. Of course, now it was connected to a disappearance, so it had to go. I drove it far north to where suburbia ceded to paddocks and dirt roads, parked it roadside, then hiked back hours to the nearest bus stop. Thanks to our wonderful transport system, I was able to return to Gray's parking lot around midnight. Fetching my own car, I drove home, where I washed out the wound to my hand.

It stung, and I imagined it would hurt worse tomorrow. Oh, that damn usurper. I wish he could feel this pain.

Still, it was a small price to pay.

## ii.

It started with the Gems – not real gems, mind you, but classic books that had fallen into the public domain, which meant anybody could now republish them. The Associates had wanted me to repackage and re-release them, to gimmick them into a series. They say you should never judge a book by its cover. Maybe that's true. What's truer is that you can sell books with really nice covers.

I met the Associates in their conference room, taking the elevator up to their floor. The elevator itself rattled and heaved in its shaft, and short-circuited if you pushed too many buttons at once. The stairs were no better – their tiling cracked and shifting treacherously – and the stairwell itself dimly lighted (particularly when the single bulb was out).

It said something that this was the way the Associates separated themselves from the rest of us employees. But that was Gray's – it was one of the oldest publishers in the world, and management liked to think of themselves as aristocracy. We employees were just the hapless court, ready to serve their every whim, while the public were their peasants.

But they were not as high and mighty as they believed. The windows in their conference room may have once overlooked a thriving coastal neighborhood full of promise back when Gray's had first been established, but time had not been kind. Now it was a pedestrian industrial sector immersed in an omnipresent murk, the ocean itself a shadowy rumpled blanket. This area had not grown as they'd anticipated half a century earlier.

The Associates themselves were just ghostly silhouettes, although I could always identify each of them by their shape and mannerisms: Randolph Lippincott, old and bent yet still the tyrannical CEO; Penelope Morgan, upright and young (at forty-five) and ambitious, ruthless; Regina Boggs, matronly, seemingly ageless, and inscrutable; Stanley Sikes, stoic, barely a shadow, rumor claimed he'd died years ago and nobody had yet realized; Kay Harlow, wheezing, decrepit, so old that time used her as a measure.

They were toweringly unimpressive once you navigated their lineage and the façade behind their mystique, although whenever I interacted with them I liked to think of them as, if nothing else, bombastic, so their whimsy fit the conceit of theatre they vainly tried to perpetuate.

"Thank you for joining us," Lippincott said grandly. "Thank you indeed. Now I won't beat around the bush: there's an opening for the role of fiction publisher. We need somebody astute to oversee our entire fiction department."

The previous fiction publisher, Barney Sacks, and I were good friends. We'd come up through school together, found jobs at Gray's together, and had often vied for the same opportunities. Some summers, we would holiday together, or indulge in retreats to sanatoriums to cleanse ourselves of all our stresses. And, occasionally, when we might've had a wine or two too many, we were convenient lovers, although he insisted it never became more than that.

Poor Barney – he had never been the strongest, nor most stable, to begin with (although he often accused me of being temperamental and impetuous). Several times, I feigned grave mental illness and would ask Barney to check himself into a mental health respite with me for the companionship and support. He thought it was him doing me the favor.

Inevitably, the workload had overwhelmed him, and he'd suffered a horrendous nervous breakdown. On this occasion, there was no need for a ruse. He voluntarily institutionalized himself, his belt and shoelaces were taken from him, and when he was unresponsive to conventional therapies, he underwent several radical, if not barbaric treatments, such as trial pharmaceuticals, electroconvulsive therapy, and a correspondence course in Scientology.

By right of succession (if there ever was such a right) his position should've been mine. I was the heir apparent for a variety of reasons – seniority, experience, and capability. But nothing was ever that simple – particularly at a multi-million-dollar publishing multinational like Gray's.

"We'd like to release a new line of books," Lippincott said. "But old ones."

"Old ones?"

"Classics," Morgan said. "Austen, Dickens, Stoker, the Brontës, and the like."

"Collectibles," Boggs said. "Something that can sit on a shelf."

"And look pretty," Morgan said.

"Do you have any ideas?" Lippincott said.

I couldn't see their faces, but I could *feel* their expectation weighing on me and *requiring* an answer that would measure up to their standards, albeit standards that were so regularly amorphous that you could never be quite sure what you were meant to say. Be too daring, and you were seen as heartlessly shattering tradition; be too traditional, and you were seen as lacking progressiveness and innovation.

But they did need this. There had been talk (there was *always* talk, but more so recently) about a hostile takeover, so the Associates often bandied about patchwork fixes, if indeed they were fixes at all. Other publishers had released similar lines such as the one the Associates were proposing. I'd have to produce something special to market these classic books into something new, shiny, and exciting.

"They're like gems," I said slowly, drawing out the sentence because I needed to stall. "Precious … and growing in value … and … sparkling … yes, sparkling gems—"

"Gems!" Lippincott said. "Brilliant. We'll take all those old classics that have fallen into the public domain and repackage them. Brightly. We need this. We need this fervently. What do you think?"

Before I could respond, Harlow interrupted with a wracking cough. Besides her antiquity, Harlow was emphysemic. Her coughing fits overpowered not only her, but the entire office, and the office building. She should've retired, or been retired, but nobody retires from Gray's – at least not voluntarily.

"I think—" I began once Harlow had ceased, but she then reverberated us with aftershocks. Finally, she fell silent, although I waited – just to be sure.

"Come along," Lippincott said. "What do you have to say?"

"I think it's a marvelous idea, sir," I said quickly, just in case Harlow set off again.

"This will take overtime outside of your other responsibilities," Lippincott said. "But do a good job, and well …" His voice trailed away, as if he expected me to guess his mind.

"Yes, sir?"

"Well, what is it we say here? There are no black and whites, no colors, only grays. But put in the time, do a good job, and you know what!"

*What* could only mean the vacant position – or why else mention it?

I set to work at once, dredging our backlists, communicating with the estates of deceased authors, as well as designers and lawyers – every-body responsible to put together the Gems. I even solicited some popular contemporary authors contracted to Gray's to write forewords for each book and then, as a novelty, commissioned them to write short stories set in the world of the book as an afterword. We released three Gems (of a planned series) in succession as big paperbacks with gold-trimmed covers, each meeting with commercial success.

When Lippincott next called me in to speak to the Associates, I was optimistic.

"You've done an exemplary job with the Gems," he said. "And those gold-trimmed pages and covers …"

The other Associates murmured their assent – all but Sikes, who seemed so insubstantial, a breath might evaporate his silhouette.

"The new fiction publisher will be pleased!" Lippincott said.

I *was* pleased.

"He will be in tomorrow."

My question of who that was exactly was lost under a salvo of Harlow's coughing.

I went home, played "Moonlight Sonata" on the piano, and tried to rationalize why they hadn't wanted me. Did they think I was too old? Or underqualified? Or overqualified? Perhaps they just liked me where I was.

Well, it wouldn't matter. Life is full of disappointments.

I would make it not matter.

### iii.

Over the next several weeks the police spoke repeatedly, but perfunctorily, with everybody – perfunctorily, because what was there to investigate? Certainly, Ivan had disappeared, but there was no real evidence of foul play; the rain had washed the parking lot clean of evidence, there were no signs of a struggle, and the company Beemer had not yet been found.

Some speculated that Ivan had absconded with the car. I recall loitering around the water-cooler (which, typically, was broken, but still the place for talk) with the other employees, and ruminating, "Do you think maybe he had a habit? Alcohol? Drugs? Gambling? Perhaps he's taken the Beemer and gone on a bender!" And then, the next thing you knew, rumors were flying around the office. However do these things begin?

"It is time we move on!" Lippincott said, when I met the Associates that morning.

"Tragic, this Ivan thing. But not to worry. We do have you."

"Yes, sir," I said.

"And we'd like to ask you … "

"Yes, sir?"

"What do you think of Nigel Bentley?"

Bentley was a contemporary, a fifty-something senior editor who'd worked for many of the multinationals. He was a friend – or he had been a friend, for many years, before time and distance and respective career trajectories had wedged us apart. But if Gray's had managed to land him, he would be quite a coup, and I told Lippincott that.

When Bentley arrived for work several days later, he embraced me and commended me extravagantly on the success of the Gems. I was naturally suspicious, sure that the praise was disingenuous, if not pointed – he wanted me to know that he believed this was my level, and he would be my superior.

Still, we fell into the begrudging rhythm of our friendship as if it had never been interrupted. We caught the train to and from work together. We had lunch together. We talked about authors, new and old, discussed and argued literature, and even empathized over poor old Barney, as if he had become a cautionary tale. And, despite his dubious opinion of me, Bentley leaned more and more on me, often dropping by my desk, asking (begging, really) for my advice on all matters publishing (and, more significantly, all things Gray's).

It justified my disgruntlement – why had this job not been mine given how much input I had into the role? It's like the Associates wanted me to be just another cog. That is the way here – everybody knows they're a cog, but one no more, or no less, significant than any other. In actual fact, Gray's perpetuates an environment of spiritual and emotional communism. Perhaps it was the Associates' way of maintaining the status quo.

I commented upon this to Bentley one chilly and misty Wednesday morning as we waited for our 7.36 am train amongst a throng of commuters.

"Yes, yes," he said, but whilst his tone was interested, his manner was distant – although that was to be expected. Bentley was in the process of an agonizing (and financially draining) separation; he'd taken this job as a means of pursuing a new start. "The Associates do exercise a form of elitism," he said. "But possibly no more than any employer."

"But I feel it deeply," I told him, as our train rumbled into the view, a silver blur punching a hole through the mist. "Particularly …"

"After the Gems?"

"Yes."

When Bentley had told me about his separation, I had felt obligated to tell him something in return – and had thus told him about the Gems, and what the Associates had implied if I carried out the task successfully.

"Really," Bentley said, "promotion isn't the be-all end-all of existence."

Of course, he would say that.

"Do not scoff, my friend!" Bentley went on. "I tell you this for your sake. You must really let it go, or it will be your un —"

I shoved Bentley as our train rattled up, the driver's eyes widening as he saw Bentley sailing in front of the windscreen. Then the awful collision. Bentley made – quite literally – a splat as the train hit him. The sound was like a hardback book hitting the floor. The curious editorial part of my mind wondered if it would've been visually similar, or if Bentley would've been flattened more like a bug on a windscreen.

But I had not much time to wonder as Bentley was lost from sight.

There was a mixture of cries from the other commuters: shouts from the more level-headed that somebody had been hit, screams from the panicked, and even a handful of astonished exclamations.

Lamentably, there was nothing to be done.

### iv.

Afterward, the police came, and asked for my account. I told them that Bentley had been distraught – his wife had left him, and he was having trouble assimilating into a new job, as well as a new town, without her. The police nodded sympathetically; they talked to colleagues, who assured them that Bentley had relied unhealthily on me, and later, I imagine they talked to his wife (sorry, ex-wife – the shrew!), who would've at least corroborated that Bentley was distraught.

"Tragic, this Bentley-thing," Lippincott said, when I met the Associates that afternoon.

"Yes, tragic."

Harlow's coughing dominated the rest of the conversation.

Unfortunately for Gray's, and several fiction publishers, the tragedies continued. Harrison Erskine, who had forty-five years' experience, was brought in from interstate to fill the vacancy left by Bentley's apparent suicide. But Erskine was only in his second day on the job when, on his way to see the Associates, he slipped down the stairs (most unfortunately, the elevator had short circuited that morning, and the single bulb in the stairwell was out) and broke his neck. Wilhelma Sorenson, a driven forty-six-year-old career editor, never even made it to work. She was the victim of a hit and run driver. Bizarrely, when police later found the car responsible, it turned out to be Ivan Kerkow's company Beemer, (and this sparked a search for him). The bullish Thomas Whitton came next. At thirty-five, and a fitness freak to boot, he thought he was invincible. But one night, just after he'd returned home and was on his way to the front door, an unknown assailant beat him to a bloody pulp – forensics later speculated it was with a sack full of blunt objects like blocks or bricks or maybe possibly even books.

Police were intrigued by the spate of misfortune that befell Gray's and here I must admit I may have inadvertently given them the impression that Barney Sacks might be responsible. When the detectives spoke to me, when they asked who might have it in for Gray's fiction publishers, who might be so "deranged", I responded, "Deranged? *Deranged?* Are you attempting to impugn Barney Sacks, the former fiction publisher, who recently had a nervous breakdown? If that's what you're trying to imply, trying to have to me acknowledge, and concede, never!"

This was a most inopportune turn of events for poor Barney. He had just been released from voluntary institutionalization, had just been given back his belt and shoelaces, but the police interrogation drove him to another breakdown, and he hung himself in his cell with his recently reacquired belt.

Poor Barney, a dangling modifier.

**V.**

First thing the next morning, the Associates summoned me. While they remained silhouettes, I could still feel their eyes upon me, keen and speculative. They may have been seeing me – truly seeing me – for the first time.

"We have had the most wretched luck," Lippincott said, "just the most wretched luck! It hasn't been very good for Sacks, Kerkow, Bentley, Erskine, Sorenson, and Whitton, either. In fact, this whole sordid affair has been very … very … very … what's the word I'm looking for?"

"Tragic?" I suggested.

"Yes! Tragic. But it now behooves us to do what we should've always done. Whilst you've been at Gray's for thirty-five years, there's been something about you lately that has impressed us, something ineffable. Well, what do you say? How would you feel about being fiction publisher?"

"I would," I began, beaming with pride, "be most magnificently, and most humbly—"

Harlow's coughing overrode the rest of my answer. I waited for it to abate, as usually it always did, but on this occasion her coughing deepened and deepened until it bounced off the walls, only to end abruptly when she keeled forward, and her face slammed into the Associates' marble table. Then she was still.

"Shit," Sikes said.

## vi.

The paramedics came almost immediately, but nothing could be done. Harlow was pronounced dead, loaded onto a gurney, covered with a sheet, and wheeled from the conference room.

I remained seated with the Associates. Death is such a rude visitor – rarely invited and often boorish. But how much death had Gray's seen recently? It was strange that this death, more than any of the others, helped contextualize what had happened and made me wonder whether it had all been worth it. We're all but stories that take on many twists, which unfold with hopefulness, and yet, inevitably, despite the happy endings that often occupy the final page, we never really know what comes after.

"I do suppose," Lippincott said, "this creates an opening, doesn't it?"

I swiveled in my chair. "An opening, you say?"

In hindsight, I think we have it about right here: when it comes to life and the choices we make, there really are no black and whites, no colors.

Only grays.

# Requiem Me

The arrival of the email shouldn't incite the dread that it does.

But maybe I've set myself up for that.

Mozart's Requiem fills the basement – a favorite of mine, but obviously not exactly upbeat. Whenever I listen to the Requiem, I think about the morbid romanticism associated with it – Mozart believing he was composing it for himself, the deathbed rehearsals, Mozart mouthing its composition with his dying breaths.

A weird countenance to that is the kids playing upstairs – they're loud and unruly and wholly oblivious. I wish Beth were here. She'd steady me, just as she always does – she is the foundation of our marriage and family, and I often tell myself I shouldn't keep casting her into that role where I need to lean on her, but I always do because she's stronger than me.

She's still at work, though.

For now, it's just me and this unopened email.

I become conscious of the Requiem again. It's the perfect accompaniment. Or maybe it's a portent.

Wait. Backstep.

I go through my extensive compilation of old CDs. They're stacked in the furthest corner of the basement, crammed together like some slipshod miniature city just waiting for Godzilla to wade through and topple it all. I've got to get better organized. But I've been saying that for years. The basement is where all the junk has migrated since Beth and I moved into this house fifteen years ago. Then my aspirations followed. And finally I came down here to chase them.

The opposite corner has been cleared for an antique mahogany desk, the shelves crammed with books about writing, a fountain pen on a jotter by a leather journal, and a desktop computer with a big, curved screen the centerpiece. Beth bought all these things for me as gifts over the years, hoping they'd help me feel writerly.

But, for right now, it's me and the CDs. I try pinpointing what'll suit the moment. Nothing. So I think about the new book I want to write, hoping that'll prompt an emotional tone. It doesn't. Not exactly, anyway. I have a character. He's a teacher. Wait, she. No, he. Well, I'll decide as I write and see what feels best. But he/she discovers that he/she has cancer (or has that been overdone?), comes home to find their partner's gone with all their things, and eventually realizes the partner didn't leave them, but was abducted. I don't know everything that happens yet. Details unveil in the writing. But I need mood music.

Pop won't work. Forget hard rock. And heavy metal's out. Oldies aren't right, although I feel my character is nostalgic. Maybe gets stuck on his/her past. The story's meant to be dark, though. Brooding. Classical – that could be it. That could hit the spot. Beethoven's Emperor Concerto. Or Mozart's Requiem. I go with the Requiem.

Then my computer chimes to signal an email's arrived.

Beth and I are in the backyard. This bit doesn't explain the email, by the way. It happened six months earlier. But it puts things in context.

We're standing by our brick barbecue. The fire's just getting going, the crackling flames shyly peeking out of the barbecue but quickly gaining gusto. The warmth feels good. It's getting on evening and a cold wind slices through the trees. Beth, leaning into me, rubs her hands together. I'm holding an accordion folder, as well as a letter I have pressed on top. The letter flaps in the wind, like a bird trying to break my grip and fly away.

"Throw it," Beth says.

I don't want to.

"It's a folder full of bad karma," Beth says.

I look at it protectively, as if I'm worried Beth might've offended it. I've had the folder for longer than I've known Beth. It's been faithful to me, and shows that by its wear – the worn seams, the creased corners, the tarnished finish. This folder's been with me my entire writing life.

Beth snatches the letter from me.

"Hey!" I say.

She scrunches it up, throws it toward the fire. I reach for it as it swirls in the wind, but it snaps away like it wants to be done with me, lands in the flames, flares, and then is gone for good.

I don't mind. It's not liberating or anything. Well, that's a lie. It's a bit liberating. Why should I carry all of it, like some burden? When I bought my accordion folder, it was light. But twenty years of filing have made it obese, although it's really me that's carrying all that extra weight. Beth knows that. She *would*. She's always been smarter than me.

"Throw it," she says.

I hold it out.

"Throw it!"

My arms sway, like I'm trying to build momentum.

"*Throw* it!"

The barbecue oomphs once the folder lands inside it. Burning twigs snap. Some of the flames desperately try to escape the folder. They don't. That's a lot of weight – a *lot* of weight. The fire wheezes, like it's struggling for breath, and belches thick black smoke. The folder's just too big and fat. It doesn't want to be killed. It wants to kill, just like the rejections it contains have tried to kill my dream.

"I'll get the kerosene," Beth says.

$$\text{\clefG}$$

That night, in bed, we fuck. Or Beth fucks me. I lie there, semi-distracted. It's wholly selfish, but sometimes I can masquerade my way through the real world while the rest of me is stuck inside my head.

I can't help but think about Mozart's Requiem – I think about it a lot when I'm down about my writing. Commissioned from Mozart by a mysterious man in black, Count Franz von Walsegg wanted it for his young, beautiful and deceased wife, Anna. The Count's plan was to pass off the Requiem as his own, but Mozart died while composing it. I wish I was that sought after. But nobody wants to steal my work. Nobody wants my work. I can't give it away.

We orgasm – well, I hope Beth does, and that she hasn't just faked it to spare me more disappointment (although that's an increasingly growing anxiety). Then we cuddle, and Beth encourages me drowsily – about the "next time", that my opportunity is "still to come", and all that great stuff she says that deep down I want to believe, and try to believe, but don't think I do – until she falls asleep.

I wonder if Mozart dealt with rejections. Rejections.

Wait. I didn't explain the folder properly.

Our house is this squat brick affair. From the street, you can see more trees than house. When Beth and I first came to see the place, Beth liked the trees – the whole area's rural – but I was ready to pass without taking a look. Beth convinced me otherwise – as always, she was patient as she waited for me to catch up. Lucky. Inside, the house was spacious, with an expansive back patio and big yard – perfect to raise our family. So it became home.

It's storming when I get home, everything blurs of grey as the rain pelts down. My intention is drive straight into the garage, but I see an A4-sized yellow envelope stuffed in the mailbox. Whoever delivered it curled it to fit into the mailbox, so it's nestled snugly, like it was some bedraggled wildlife that crept in there for shelter.

Crap. Hang on. Forgot something again.

We sit at the dinner table – me at one end, Beth at the other, the kids to either side of us. The kids aren't important, though. I mean obviously they are to us, but for the purpose of what I'm telling you, they're not important. They're just context.

I pick at my peas, prodding them, one by one.

"It's good," Beth says.

"What?" I ask. I know. But I want to hear it. *Need* to.

Beth's eyes flit to the counter. On it is a yellow A4-sized envelope that contains three chapters of a new novel I've just finished revising – "Ice Like Fire" – as well as a cover letter and a stamped self-addressed envelope. That's everything stipulated in the submission guidelines of Gray's Publishing. I've been around long enough, and had enough experiences, to know that you should always give a publisher exactly what they want – it shows professionalism. I wonder how professional Mozart was. Stories abound that he was irreverent, if not immature at times. Then again, he was a prodigy, composing and performing when he was a kid. I'm still trying to break through in middle age.

"You confident?" Beth says.

That's enough of this digression, actually, and you don't want to hear my whining self-doubt. Beth has to deal with that enough.

Anyway, the envelope in the mailbox is the stamped self-addressed envelope.

It's my envelope.

Stupid envelope.

I take out the envelope and weigh it in my hand. It feels exactly the weight of the one I sent, which means it must contain my three chapters.

Once upon a time, I would have deluded myself into thinking that the envelope contained good news. I'd pause and relish the anticipation. There would be a letter in the envelope saying, *We love these three chapters — send us the rest!* Of course, that's illogical. If they wanted to see more, they could phone, email, or send just a letter back. They wouldn't also be sending back my chapters.

I tear open the envelope, find a small square sheet inside it amid my three chapters. I pull it out. The letter has the masthead of Gray's Publishing on the top, under which is a form response. They address me as "Dear Author" and tell me that while they read my work with interest, it's not quite what they're looking for. They wish me the best in the future.

I stomp into the basement, turn on the light and, just before I flick on the radio, tell myself that whatever song comes on will be a portent.

It's Michael Jackson's "I Just Can't Stop Loving You." No relevance at all. Bloody song.

Sitting at my antique desk, I lean back in my chair and – damn it – I feel writerly. It's the immediate environment. The feng shui. Just as Beth planned it. Everything conspires to make me feel writerly – other than me, that is.

Underneath my desk is a small set of drawers. I open the bottom drawer, and there looking up at me like an expectant dog wanting a treat, is my accordion folder. I am about to file away my latest rejection, when I lean back in my chair and look at the rejection again, some imbecilic hope sparking that maybe, just maybe, I read it wrong.

Nope.

That leaves the reality to charge in and crush me.

Gray's took six months to reject me – six months where I told myself not to build my hopes up, but I did. You can't help it. They build – quietly and secretly – in some dim niche of your mind. Like an aneurysm.

Hands close on my shoulders. It's Beth. I lean back into her massage.

"You can try again someplace else," she says.

I shrug.

"The first *Harry Potter* was rejected umpteen times. You know that."

"Maybe it's just not meant to happen."

"That's the rejection talking."

"It's been talking a long time."

"Don't listen."

I snort.

Beth's hands fall from my shoulders. I think about our lives together: almost twenty years married (we married young), two houses (one rental!) whose mortgages we're struggling to pay off, three kids (one diabetic, one dyslexic – okay, maybe they're a bit important), me the floor manager at a tech warehouse while Beth is the fundraising supervisor for a foundation researching various cancers (both jobs where we hit career ceilings years earlier, but remain there because they pay the bills). And we're sitting here, end-of-the-world talk, because my hobby's not paying off.

"Come on," Beth says. "Take the rejection. And that folder."

"What?"

"Grab them. Now."

"But—"

"Now."

I take the folder out of the drawer.

"Let's go," Beth says.

"Where?"

"Let's go."

I don't ask again.

Beth and I are in the backyard. The fire's soaring now. I worry about sparks drifting up into the trees and starting a blaze. Who would've thought an accordion folder full of rejections would burn so well? Okay, that and enough kerosene to launch a rocket. The kids watch from the windows of the house, probably wondering why parents who constantly lecture them about responsibility and fire safety around trees are behaving so recklessly.

"Feel better?" Beth asks.

"What about the next one?"

"If there's a next one, we'll deal with it then."

"With fire?"

"A fire, an exorcism, whatever works best. Then we'll move on. Move forward."

"I'm moving sideways with this. Or maybe not even sideways. Maybe spiraling. Like water down a drain. Maybe I just don't know it yet."

"Maybe maybe maybe. You write well. 'Ice Like Fire' is a good read. It'll happen."

"I don't know anymore."

"I believe in you. *You* just need to believe in you."

"How do I do that after all this time?"

"Tell me, do you think it's worth it?"

"Is it for you? I mean, supporting me and everything while I whine and have these crises of self-confidence and everything?"

"It *is*," Beth says. "That's why I keep pushing you, keep supporting you – because I know you have the talent if you just believe." She grows thoughtful, although I know she's already decided on something. "Maybe you need to take a little break," she says.

"So you can throw maybes around?"

Beth stands on her tiptoes and kisses me. "Tonight, I'll get your mind off it."

"How?"

She smiles.

So I lie in bed, thinking about Mozart. Did he ever question his ability when he was bumming around, begging friends for loans? Did he ever wonder whether people would enjoy his music? What would've happened to him if he'd bombed out time and again? Would he have considered getting out? Maybe getting a real job, selling door-to-door encyclopedias or something? I can't picture him still trying at forty – not that he lived that long. But maybe he would've directed his energies elsewhere.

I decide that's what I should do.

I don't, though.

Fast forward.

It's five a.m. Have fast-forwarded a whole four hours. You probably expected more.

Sorry.

I sit in the basement, in pajama bottoms and a bathrobe, shivering, as I Google publishers I haven't tried yet. There's one, Palette. It's small.

Boutique. Whereas Gray's is a multinational. Also, Gray's is interstate. Palette is local. I could drive there in fifteen minutes. There goes that nook of my mind – hoping, dreaming. I see myself sitting in a meeting with Palette as we talk about my book. We talk about it, because obviously they've accepted it. So it's convenient that they're local. Because I could drive down there. See?

I check their website. They request the entire book, a cover letter, a bio and a CV (if applicable). All these things are ready on my computer to print. The book I'll print from scratch, even though I still have the first three chapters that Gray's returned. But those three chapters are tainted. Better to get rid of them rather than risk letting them pollute this endeavor.

Then I see a note on the Palette website from the new head of their fiction department that says they've gone green, meaning they won't accept hardcopy. Everything's done via email, which makes everything quick and easy – no having to slip out of work during my lunch hour to get to the post office; no having to dread stamped self-addressed envelopes turning up in my mailbox like prospective letter bombs.

I attach all the requested files to an email, paste in a covering letter, type "Submission: Ice Like Fire – A Commercial Novel" in the subject line, and hit SEND.

I am an idiot for doing this.

$$\text{\textipa{𝄞}}$$

So, I stare at the email sitting unopened in my mailbox. I've already been staring a while now. The Sequentia of Mozart's Requiem unfolds. The kids are raucous upstairs, like they're ritualizing the moment into something ceremonial. But it's not about them.

It's about the email.

It's from Palette Publishing.

The subject line reads "Re: Submission: Ice Like Fire -A Commercial Novel."

There's no way to tell – without reading it – if it's a rejection. There are no clues with an email.

So I stare some more.

While it sits unopened, there's hope. It's not that I want to savor the anticipation. In a way, it's not enjoyable. It's too tense to be enjoyable. But while it exists, it validates my dreams, lets me believe that all things are possible, that this is finally it.

The Requiem still fills the basement, although I've played it so often it's coated onto the walls in more layers than the paint.

As I often do, I immerse myself in the sublime perfection of the music. Think now about how Mozart worked on it until his death, even as he feared he was writing his own requiem. The day before he died, friends came over to sing parts of the Requiem for him. In his last hours, he was mouthing it.

It's then that I realize it doesn't matter what's in the email.

It doesn't matter how whatever it contains makes me feel.

Nothing matters but what I want to do until the very end.

I open the email.

# Acknowledgements

These stories reflect my writing and publishing experiences, albeit with some embellishment. (I'll let you work out where that's occurred.)

The first drafts were written years ago: *The Slush Pile Demolitionist* in August 2008, *Promotion* in October 2008, and *Requiem Me* in October 2011. But they've been redrafted exhaustively (if not obsessively) since then.

I've also gotten feedback from lots of great feedbackers (who are great writers in their own right), so a big thank you to Blaise van Hecke, Therese Mobayad, Ryan O'Neill, Laurie Steed, Barry Carozzi, Andrew Morgan, Rob Deskoski, Tom O'Connell, Skye Blake, Belinda Woods, and Kim Lock.

Also, a thank you to the editors where these stories were originally published: *The Slush Pile Demolitionist* in the *Dillydown Prize Anthology* (May 2022), and read on season 4, episode 11, of the literary podcast *Nobody Reads Short Stories*, *Promotion* in *Blue Crow Magazine* (April 2010), and *Requiem Me* in *Etchings* (Issue 11, 2012).

Thanks to my obsessiveness, these redrafts of *Promotion* and *Requiem Me* are quite different from their original published forms.

# About the Author

Les Zig has loved storytelling in all its forms his whole life.

He believes in stories where the reader takes a journey right alongside the characters, and together they experience lows, highs, adventures, failures, and triumphs.

His own writing attempts to explore the boundaries of human aspiration and desires, and while navigating serious themes employs the occasional irreverence that we see every day. What is life without humor?

He has five published novels (listed overleaf), had stories and articles printed extensively, and also written and directed screenplays.

He has a website, www.leszig.com, where you can learn more about him.

# Other novels by Les Zig …

Pantera Press
*August Falling*
*Just Another Week in Suburbia*

ECG Press
*Prudence*

## As Lazaros Zigomanis …

MidnightSun Publishing
*This*

ECG Press
*Song of the Curlew*
*The Shadow in the Wind*

Busybird Publishing
*Pride*